WHAT [ ] THE CROCODILE SAY?

Eva Montanari

BOOK ISLAND

THE ALARM CLOCK
GOES DRINGG DRINGG.

THE TICKLE GOES HEE HEE.

THE WATER GOES SSSPLASH.

THE ZIP GOES ZZZUP.

THE BREAKFAST GOES MUNCH.

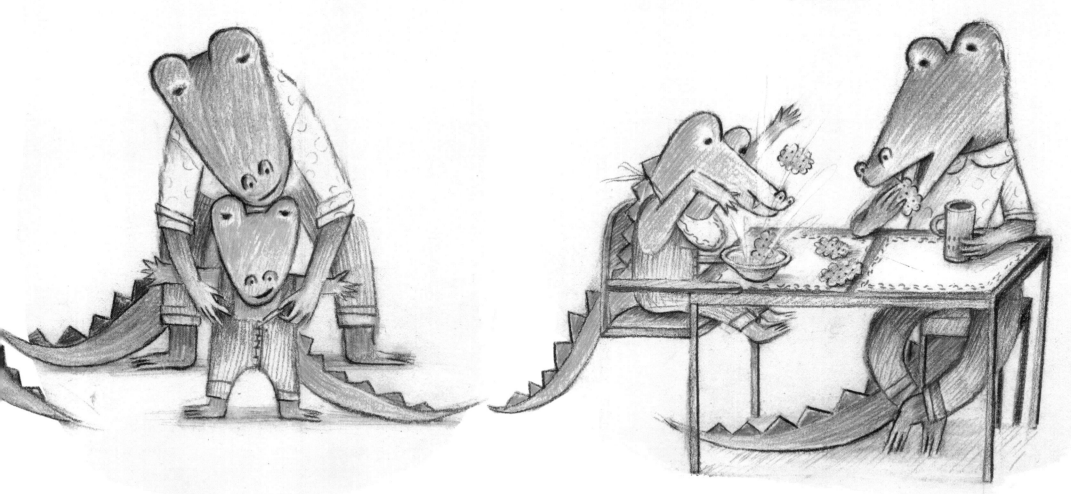

THE CAR GOES VROOM VROOM.

THE CAR DOOR
GOES BLEEP.

THE BELL GOES
DING DONG.

THE ELEPHANT SAYS PEEKABOO.

THE STAIRS GO HUP HUP.

THE PIG SAYS OINK OINK.
THE CAT SAYS MEOW.
THE BIRD SAYS TWEET TWEET.
THE FROG SAYS RIBBIT RIBBIT.
THE MONKEY SAYS
OOOH OOOH
AAAH AAAH.

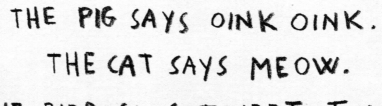

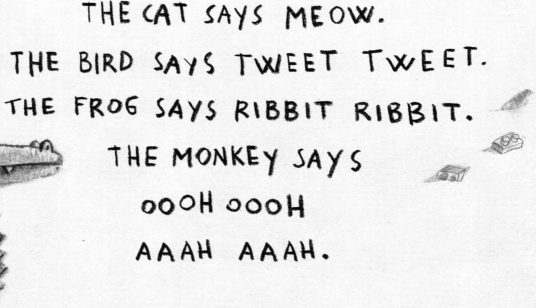

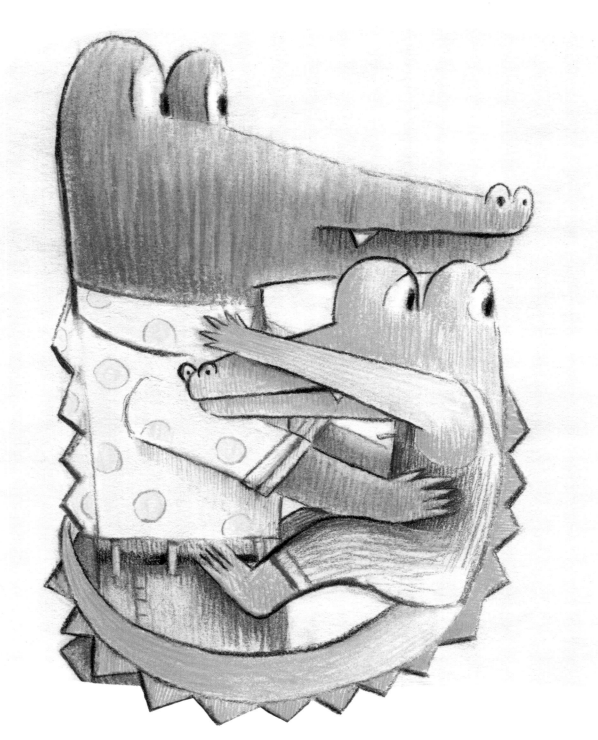

AND WHAT DOES
THE CROCODILE
SAY?

THE BOOK GOES
"ONCE UPON A TIME..."

THE DRUM GOES
POM-PA-POM
POM-PA-POM
POM-PA-POM.

THE TRUMPET
GOES
TOOT TOOT.

THE
TRIANGLE
GOES
TINGG.

THE FOOD GOES
OM OM OM.

THE MILK GOES
GLUG GLUG.

THE NAP GOES ZZZ ZZZ

ZZZ ZZZ.

MAMA SAYS PEEKABOO.

AND WHAT
DOES THE
CROCODILE
SAY ?

MWAH

MWAH

MWAH

MWAH

MWAH

MW

MWAH

THE GOODBYE GOES

"SEE YOU TOMORROW!"

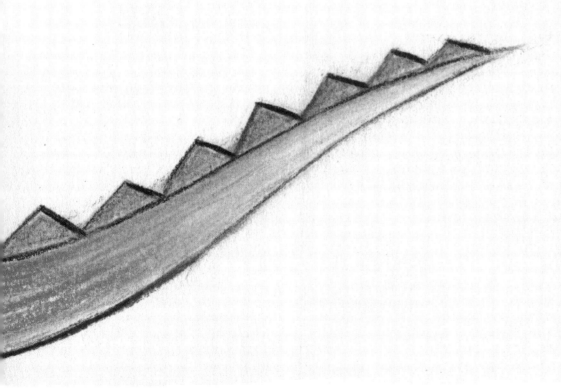